for my mum,
and her chameleon

Text and Illustrations © Emily Gravett 2010
ISBN: 978-0-330-51875-8

1 3 5 7 9 8 6 4 2

Printed in China

A CIP catalogue record for this book is available from the British Library

Blue
Chameleon

Emily Gravett

Macmillan Children's Books

Blue chameleon

Yellow

banana

Pink

cockatoo

Swirly

snail

Brown

boot

Stripy

sock

Spotty

ball

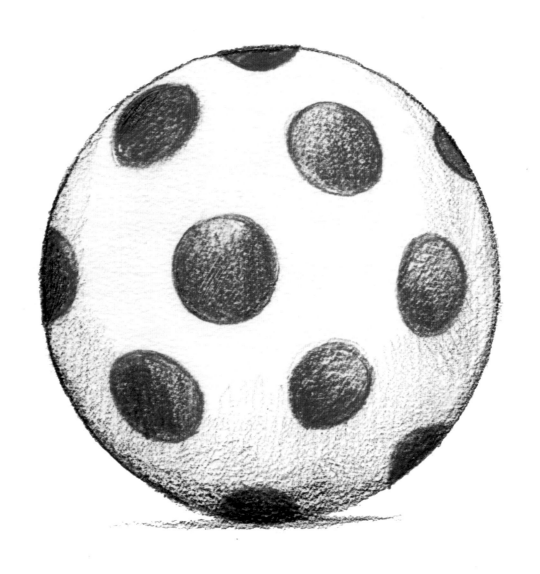

Gold

fish

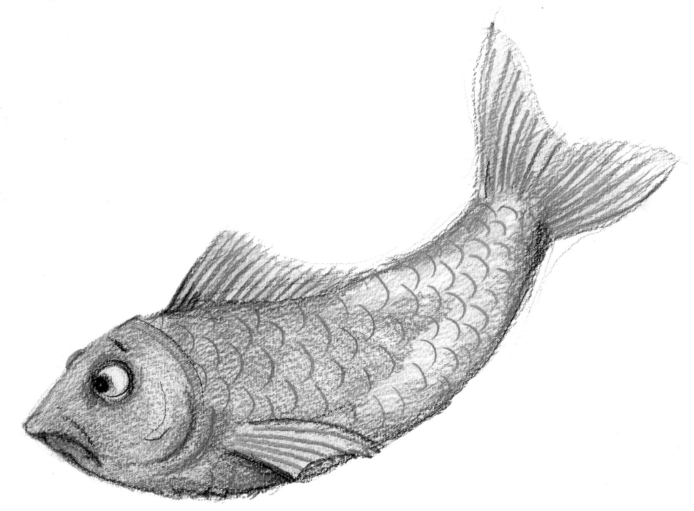

Green
grasshopper

Grey

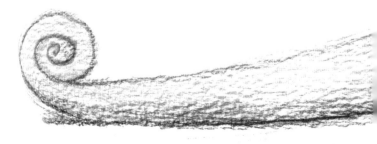

rock

White

page

Colourful

chameleons